Expansion Upon a Theme

A Short Erotic Tale of Two BBW Lesbians

By Molly Weisser

DEDICATION

To all who share in the pleasure and affirmation in erotic weight gain kink community.

DESCRIPTION

Stephanie, a professional art collector and investor, always gets what she wants. And when she meets college student Kelsey one hot summer day, she discovers that her great need for a protégé will be met with hunger and eagerness.

This story is a quasi-realistic piece of lesbian BBW erotic weight gain fiction involving the following elements: Extreme weight gain (200lbs+), Feeder/feedee relationship, Intentional erotic weight gain, Kissing, Oral sex. A modern-day lesbian BBW/BBW romance with food fetishization and weight-gain kinkiness. Written as a commission for D.M. and published with permission.

A HUSBAND FOR ADSILA

It was hot and crowded in the central plaza at San Miguel park, and Stephanie was grumpy. While she was pleasantly surprised at the caliber of art vendors at this fair, she'd just discovered a telltale hole in her size-thirty-odd denim shorts, and her thighs no longer had cushioning against the inevitable chub rub. This leisurely walk from her car was suddenly unendurable. Her sweat was making everything worse, and she could feel the drips running down her shapely calves. Even her camisole top was surrendering to the wet Florida heat; it appeared limp and decidedly not as attractive as it had in the comfort of her air-conditioned bedroom.

Finally, she spotted her destination: her friend Lupe's fine arts booth.

"Ugh," she exhaled, and poured her massive, well-rounded body into the offered Hercules chair. Thank god it was cloth so her too-luscious thighs wouldn't stick to the pleather. "You got anything cold, Loop?"

"I gotchu, chica," Lupe smiled, and leaned down to reach into an ice chest near her feet. "What you want, water or iced tea?"

"You got any soda?" Stephanie grumbled, and she grabbed a napkin tucked under a paper plate with the remnants of Lupe's lunch. She used this to dab at her temples, which were shiny with perspiration.

"Ay, gorda," Lupe answered, rolling her eyes. "Like you need all that sugar."

"That's no way to treat your best customer," Stephanie bit out, trying to smile and pretend she wasn't angry. Like she'd *asked* for Lupe's opinion.

"Oh mamacita," Lupe replied, shining brightly at Stephanie through her too-heavy mascara. "You know I'm just joking. You know I love you."

"Yeah." Stephanie received the diet root-beer without commentary. She desperately needed something to boost her blood sugar, and moreover she hated the taste of aspartame, but she wasn't going to say anything else on the subject. Not when she'd been so swiftly shut down for no good reason.

This was why Stephanie *hated* to mix friends and business. She took a chance once in a while, when she forgot how odious it was to try and collect on her investments. And every time, like clockwork, people kept trying to take advantage of her, and she was fucking sick of it.

She closed her eyes and tried to calm her accelerating pulse. Wouldn't do anyone any good for her to get worked up about this. Lupe was worth it - she could feel it in her bones that Lupe was going to make it big, with the right backing. It just was so hard to get people to stop treating her like a milk cow once they started.

After returning to her previous state of relative tranquility, Stephanie opened her eyes to scan over the rest of the show - a.k.a. The Competition.

Instead, however, her attention was immediately captured by a vision of incredible elegance: a young woman with long brown hair and incredible, penetrating brown eyes. And confusingly, she was wearing the same purple smock that Lupe also wore.

"What, you got rid of Jane?" Stephanie asked of Lupe, and she couldn't help but smile broadly at the other girl.

"No, she's helping her brother at Coachella," Lupe answered, a distinctive hint of disdain in her voice. "This is Kelsey, another one of my students."

"Hey," Kelsey said, her eyes wide. "Nice to meet you."

She extended her hand, which was covered in dried paint splatter, but Stephanie didn't comment on it. It had been a long while since she'd seen someone so damn *cute.* It almost scared her, how suddenly and instantly she wanted this girl. No sooner than Kelsey turned around did Stephanie find herself ogling: an adorable bubble-butt that begged to balloon, thighs so thick and strong that Stephanie could imagine *exactly* how heavenly they tasted, and the emergence of love-handles that poked with light skin from underneath the slightly-too-small tank-top.

The girl was extremely touchable, but there was something somewhat unfinished about her. Like ice cream that was kept in the freezer too long, and needed to thaw a little bit more before consumption.

Stephanie, while she deeply appreciated art, was not much of an artist herself. But to look at Kelsey, she felt a surge of creative inspiration unlike she ever had felt before. At first, she was confused by the sensation, but then as she contemplated Kelsey's fine posterior, with jeans that looked pasted on and back pockets that simply begged for another woman's hands to slip inside.... Well, suffice it to say, she figured it out.

She wanted to sculpt Kelsey - and sculpt her into a very well-fed version of herself. Stephanie could practically see it, like an architect looking at a vacant lot and imagining a house there. Kelsey would look absolutely *fabulous* if she were proportionally much more similar to Stephanie herself - heavy breasts, engorged stomach, beautiful hips that went on for days…

The thought of Kelsey looking so gorgeous made Stephanie wet, and not just with sweat. Her breathing quickened, and she felt a burgeoning need growing in her nether regions.

To hide her nervousness, she checked her makeup in her phone's camera. Her eyeliner was on point, her blonde hair was a little deflated with sweat but at least it still looked okay, and her bright pink lipstick required just the slightest touchup.

"So, Lupe," Stephanie asked as Kelsey sauntered away to wash some paintbrushes in the bathroom, "Kelsey - what kind of men she into?"

Lupe rolled her eyes. "If you think I'm gonna hire a *straight* chick to represent my brand, mamacita? You cray-cray."

"Oh, okay," Stephanie said, trying to hide her interest by burying her nose in her cell phone. After a pregnant moment, she asked, "You think she's seeing anyone?"

"I don't keep track of that shit," Lupe shrugged, "but if you want, I'll give her your number."

"Yeah," Stephanie said, and she struggled to her feet. The ponderous heaviness of her four-hundred-forty-odd body was getting the best of her these days, in the dating scene. "If she likes fat girls, that is."

"You tell me what you think she likes," Lupe said, and with distaste she picked up the piece of art that Kelsey had been working on. It was, to Stephanie's ecstatic delight, a nude watercolor portrait of a woman that likely weighed more than Stephanie.

"Who's the model?" Stephanie asked, astonished at the way Kelsey had captured the highly-realistic-looking curves and contours of the human form.

"She said it was that lady," Lupe said, gesturing with her wrist as she leaned down to grab herself a soda.

Stephanie's eyes glanced over the populace and noticed the sight of a plain-looking, exceptionally rotund older woman sitting on a park bench, eating an entire quart of ice cream and staring with appreciation at the kids on the playground.

Hm. Talented enough to draw mostly from imagination for her art, inspired by a real-life vision of what Stephanie herself expected to look like in a few years? Stephanie liked her chances with this girl.

Now to reel her in.

. . . .

Soon enough, Stephanie was sitting in the center of her posh living-room, trying not to let her nerves take over. She had the television on to a cooking show, but she held the remote in her hand, ready to mute it at any moment.

Then, at precisely seven o'clock (as if her guest had been standing at the door of the apartment staring at her watch) the doorbell rang.

Stephanie, in her infinite laziness, had installed an automatic door-opening system so she wouldn't have to get up too fast. So she switched it on, and she stood up from the couch, looking as regal and unhurried as a queen.

"Heyyyy," Kelsey said, looking a tiny bit awestruck. "You live at the Palermo Tower? I've always wanted to come here."

She looked just the same as she had that afternoon, less her purple apron, plus a pretty horrific sunburn across her neck, shoulders, and arms. It was quite cute, and a bit amusing as well.

"It's pretty sweet," Stephanie said, and gestured to the couch opposite her. The air-conditioning was on full-blast, the couches were carefully brushed for pet hair from her cat, and there was something delicious in the oven from Montclair's restaurant. She felt the image of the successful and elegant self-employed woman that she always projected outside her home. "Sit back, relax. Have a mimosa."

"It's a bit late for mimosa," observed Kelsey, but she took one anyway.

"I'm of the opinion that in Florida, any time is mimosa time," Stephanie said, trying not to let her smile falter.

Kelsey looked embarrassed. "I mean, I agree," she said, seeming ashamed for having said anything. "I don't know why I said that. Sorry. I don't mean to be impolite."

"Oh sweetie, you're fine," Stephanie cooed, and she gently got up and reseated herself closer to Kelsey, just close enough their sandals might accidentally brush under the coffee table if they weren't careful. "You're *fine.*" She emphasized this last word with a heavy dose of flirtatiousness, and she felt her mouth watering just to look at the other girl.

Then she thought of an idea.

"Would you like something for that sunburn?" she murmured, and without waiting for an answer, she added, "I have some fresh aloe vera on the patio here."

"No, no need to trouble yourself," Kelsey said, but Stephanie was already mobile and walking away from the living room - making positively sure that her hips sashayed with every step. She stepped out onto the balcony, broke off a chunk of aloe leaf where it grew in a pot, and then she was back inside, closing the door firmly behind her.

Stephanie was pleasantly surprised at the way Kelsey's eyes traced Stephanie's entire body from head to toe, and the way Kelsey seemed especially enchanted by the way Stephanie's voluptuous form jiggled with every high-heeled step.

"Here we go," Stephanie said, and approached Kelsey from behind. "Would you mind if I apply it for you?"

"Please...erm...go ahead," Kelsey said, her ears flushing dramatically pink. "That'd be fine."

With that, Stephanie began to apply the silicone-smooth nectar of the aloe plant upon the burned and raw skin of the beautiful woman who sat upon her couch. Her fingers were soft and strong, well-practiced in the art of massage after years of doing this work professionally. Nowadays she was too obese to do it on a daily basis, particularly things that required a lot of upper-arm strength, but she didn't mind indulging someone in an intimate setting once in a while.

Actually, Stephanie wanted to touch Kelsey badly, and all over. Her fingers ached to play with the girl's well-softened chub that hung along the line of her latissimus dorsi, to truly knead at the girl's buttery trapezial area, and to better assess the decadent curves of her buttocks.

Fortunately, Stephanie had a plausible excuse ready-made. "I can't really get it all while you're on the couch," Stephanie said, feeling sinfully temptatious. "Would you like to come to my work bench?"

Kelsey looked a little confused, and turned her head painfully to meet Stephanie's eyes.

"I have a massage table," Stephanie clarified and Kelsey nodded.

"Sure, let's do it," Kelsey said, though her breath was a little bit caught in her throat, as if she knew this were all a ruse.

Not that Stephanie minded. All the better if Kelsey was walking into the situation with both eyes open.

The women went into Stephanie's workroom, and Kelsey was clearly impressed at the sights. A little fountain, dim LED lighting, and gorgeous art created a peaceful tableaux.

"I see some of Professor Martinez' work," Kelsey said, appearing titillated at the sight of Lupe's art on Stephanie's walls. "It looks better here than it does in the gallery, honestly."

"You know I'm her chief investor," Stephanie said, a little stern. Kelsey turned, eyes wide, and quickly she flagellated herself.

"I didn't mean- ugh-"

"Hey," Stephanie said with a laugh, and she patted the massage table invitingly. "Cool it, babe."

Looking nervous, Kelsey began to unsnap her jeans. Then, with a shudder of realization, as Stephanie's eyes warmly appreciated the sight of Kelsey's little belly pooching over her waistband, Kelsey gasped, "Erm, do you want me to wear my underwear or…"

"What do you usually do?" Stephanie asked, curious.

"Normally al fresco, so to speak," Kelsey responded, looking a little embarrassed.

"Then al fresco it is," Stephanie cooed, and she broke open the aloe a little higher up the stalk. "I promise I'll keep my hands to myself. Now hurry up. I can't stand as long as I used to, thanks to my fat ass."

Kelsey swallowed visibly, as if suppressing desire. But she didn't say anything, and instead took the towel that Stephanie reluctantly offered. It was clear that she didn't have much use for modesty, though; she barely bothered to unfold it, much less hold it against her sumptuous breasts.

Ah, young women these days. While Stephanie wasn't more than ten years older than Kelsey, she did feel old in some ways. It had taken a lot more convincing to get Stephanie's clothes completely off, back in the day.

Not that Stephanie minded, not one bit.

Soon enough, Kelsey was flat on the table, her round buttocks perky and orblike, cresting over the rest of her body like the sun peeking over a hill.

While her buttocks were not burned at all, Stephanie was pleased to notice that Kelsey's midriff hadn't been spared. Plausible deniability, right there, waiting. She would get there eventually, but first she had to pretend like she wasn't just a horny son-of-a.

"I don't give a shit what you think of Lupe's work," Stephanie went on, as Kelsey shuddered at the cool gel encountering her tense shoulders, "I think she's got about as much talent as you have in your little finger."

"You- what?" asked Kelsey, sounding puzzled.

"I saw that watercolor you were working on, in the park," Stephanie said, hoping her voice was oozing sensuality. "I couldn't help but admire your handiwork."

"It was just a quick sketch," Kelsey said self-effacingly, "not like something I worked very hard on. I mean," she went on, and she sounded very embarrassed. "I kinda did that just for… erm… myself."

"All the more reason to admire it," Stephanie said, though none of this was exactly news to her. "For that drawing alone, my dear, I could get a buyer to pay you five hundred bucks. Easy."

"For real?" asked Kelsey, sounding astonished. "For a watercolor?"

"Yeah," Stephanie answered, allowing her fingers to sink a little lower on Kelsey's back. "It's all about the market, honey. And your market is *hungry.*"

"You mean, the market for fat ladies in the nude?" asked Kelsey, still incredulous.

"Damn straight," Stephanie said, and then laughed a little. "I suppose I should say, 'damn queer.'" She began to massage Kelsey's midriff.

Kelsey laughed, and it was genuine - Stephanie's poor joke notwithstanding. Her body rippled deliciously, with all the suggestiveness of a pudding, and Stephanie nearly swooned at the sight.

She required a few moments of quiet contemplation to recover. But her courage was soaring.

"Do you mind if I go a little lower?" Stephanie added, once the skin just above the buttocks was saturated.

"Be my guest," mumbled Kelsey, sounding deliriously happy. "Oh my god, this was just what I needed. Fuck."

Stephanie, reading Kelsey's clear signals, ran her fingers across Kelsey's delicious rump. The skin wobbled and flexed with the motion of a water bed, and it was all she could do not to slap Kelsey's behind with a broad hand. She settled for patting it, and then, once she'd paid enough attention to that wonderful body part, her fingers kept wandering down Kelsey's thighs.

She felt Kelsey's hamstrings passionately tensing, which suggested one of several things - most likely stress or discomfort, but very *possibly* pleasure.

This last hypothesis was confirmed by Kelsey's asking, with a little fear in her voice, "Could you, erm, are you going to do the blooming rose?"

"The what?" Stephanie had never heard of such a thing.

"I… erm, sorry, forget it," Kelsey mumbled from her pillow, probably glad she didn't have to make eye contact.

Stephanie did have an idea of what this 'blooming rose' business was, but she wasn't going to make it easy for this little dumpling girl who was so eager to unfurl.

"I'm going to try a few things," Stephanie said in a low, seductive voice, trying not to let herself squeak with eagerness. "You tell me if I get it right, okay hun?"

"Erm, okay," Kelsey responded, sounding a little curious and possibly scared.

"Before I start," Stephanie added, running her pudgy fingers up and down Kelsey's spine, "is there any area on your body I should *not* touch?"

"Not that I can think of," Kelsey said, after a moment's hesitation.

"Are you *sure?*" Stephanie was thrilled to basically have carte blanche with the other girl's body.

Kelsey nodded as best she could while being face-down. "Yeah," she uttered, her voice rough and hoarse, as if she knew exactly what she was getting into.

All the better. Stephanie couldn't take it anymore, anyway. She allowed her fingers to plunge deeply into Kelsey's vaginal channel, without any warning, and Kelsey gave a little yelpy moan.

"There we go, my dear," Stephanie murmured sweetly. She felt her own thighs growing sticky with lust, but that didn't matter. Kelsey was well on her way to cumming all over the massage table. Already Stephanie could see the woman tensing up every muscle of her body, and she heard the way Kelsey gasped and shuddered with every perfect stroke. "That's it. Come to mama."

And with an exhausted gasp, Kelsey came - splendidly and naturally, her entire body convulsing and aching as she felt the orgasm shake through her body.

Stephanie was ready for the second round, but Kelsey raised a hand to stop her.

"I only do one," she gasped, raising her head up from the table. She was beaming ear to ear. "At least until you've also had one."

Before Stephanie knew it, the women tumbled into her bedroom, scarcely able to turn the lights on and tear their clothes off.

Kelsey had the advantage of already being naked, of course, but she valiantly attempted to persuade Stephanie's body-con dress off. It ended up requiring Stephanie's assistance as well, which made Kelsey breathe very heavily at the sight of Stephanie's ponderous arm-fat dangling in the air.

"You like that?" Stephanie asked, panting with the effort of rushing through her deshabille.

"Erm, yeah," Kelsey admitted, and she grabbed Stephanie by her now bare waist and wrestled the heavy woman onto the bed. "You're so fucking gorgeous. I've been so turned on all day thinking about coming over."

"You are too, my dear," Stephanie murmured, and she pressed a hot, passionate kiss into Kelsey's surprised lips. "Damnit. You really are."

However, her 'but' seemed to hang in the air. At first, Kelsey didn't seem to notice it, but after a few more minutes of frenzied kissing, the two of them pulled away from each other, giggling a little bit.

"I feel like there's something you're not quite satisfied with, though," Kelsey said, smirking at the way Stephanie rolled her eyes in response.

"It's not a big deal," Stephanie said, though she was being strategically coy.

"No, come on," Kelsey insisted, and she propped up her head on her hand. "You can tell me. Come on. What is it?"

"It's just…" Stephanie sighed. She allowed herself to look a little vulnerable for a moment, but then she retreated again. "No. It's not okay. I just met you. What the hell am I thinking?"

"Well come on, tell me!" Kelsey encouraged, and her hand began to wend its way down Stephanie's pillow-soft thigh.

"I can't," Stephanie begged, though it was obvious at this point she was about to relent.

But she just needed one more piece to fall into place…

…and there it was. Kelsey's finger was toying with her clit, *finally,* and she now could relax into her vision.

"Oh god," she breathed with a gasp, and that was entirely genuine. "Oh god. Well."

She took a deep breath and tried to frame her question as delicately as possible.

"So I have to confess," Stephanie breathed, her pulse quickening, "I'm not an artist. Not really. But once in awhile I do sculpting, of a kind."

Kelsey's head quirked curiously, but she said nothing, just waiting for Stephanie to finish elaborating. Kelsey's hand was warm and remained solidly between Stephanie's thick labia petals, and with every breath Kelsey took, Stephanie could feel Kelsey's fingers palpitating against her clit.

"Oh my god, I can't believe I'm telling you this," Stephanie obfuscated, blushing furiously. That was genuine, even if she had been planning all along to tell Kelsey her morbid desires. "Okay, here goes."

She felt her vagina muscles flex involuntarily, but also her throat.

"Well. I confess that when I first saw you… I kinda realized that you weren't living up to your fullest potential."

Well that wasn't the most subtle way she'd ever seduced a young lady into gaining before, but it came close.

Kelsey, making no assumptions, raised a curious eyebrow and waited for further explanation.

"You *really* could stand to gain a little weight," Stephanie stated, and she cupped one hand around Kelsey's perky, petite little breast. "I mean, come on. Don't you see that your body is just *aching* to bloom? Your ass, it quakes. Your stomach, it ripples. Your breasts, they pop. But oh god, they could be *so much more.* Don't you see?"

Kelsey thought for a while. "I actually do," Kelsey replied slowly, "and I've often thought so myself. My stomach is plump, but I've always wanted to be really *rotund* like you." She giggled self-consciously. "But I've never tried to put on any weight. Mostly worried about other people's reactions."

"Well, let's say you say what I say," Stephanie said, and grinned like a wolf. "Fuck 'em."

"All right," Kelsey said, seeming pensive. And at first Stephanie was waiting for a further decision to be made - but then Kelsey said, "So, what are you waiting for, hm?"

"Oh!" Stephanie responded, eyes wide and shining with lust. "Nothing. I'll be right back."

She practically skipped out of the room, naked and all.

. . . .

"What the hell is this?" Kelsey said, looking at the bottle. "Weight gain pills?"

"Yeah," Stephanie said, and rolled her eyes. "Look, we'll go slow, all right?"

"Okay," Kelsey said, and frowned, reading the label. "Ten pounds per pill?"

"That's what they say," Stephanie said, and patted her own large tummy. "While I got to my current size all on my own, once in a while I take 'em if I accidentally lose a few pounds due to stress."

"Where do you even get something like this?" Kelsey asked, and she looked very curious. "This can't be legal."

"If you don't want to, we don't have to," Stephanie said, but the tone of her voice implied clearly: "but if you don't want to, I won't want you."

"Oh no, I do want to," Kelsey amended quickly. "Just like… how did you get these?"

Stephanie winked. "That's for me to know, darling, and you to never find out."

Kelsey just groaned. "Okay, well, I just hope it doesn't hurt."

"It won't hurt, sweetie," Stephanie cooed, and she patted the bed tenderly. "Let's get you into something a little more comfortable, though."

So saying, she tossed one of her own 4xl mumus to Kelsey, who grinned and slipped inside. "You think I'm going to actually fill this up?" she asked, and a shudder of pleasure ran through her body.

"Maybe not *all* the way," Stephanie said, but she winked. "I do like to be larger than my partners, generally."

Kelsey flushed, and lay back on the silk pillows, opening her mouth eagerly.

Stephanie offered Kelsey some soda, and four pills. Kelsey sipped and swallowed, and closed her eyes.

Stephanie never had the pleasure of seeing someone really use the pills like this. Kelsey's body seemed to practically inflate, at first just the tiniest bit, but then all of a sudden the active ingredients seemed to metabolize, and Kelsey suddenly had a nice, plump belly, which plopped out in front of her in the very picture of a spare tire.

"Very good," Stephanie surveyed, and before Kelsey could protest, Stephanie was down in Kelsey's plump cunt, licking and sucking with a passionate frenzy.

"Oh god, god, GOD!" screamed Kelsey as she orgasmed fast and hard, so powerfully it was almost as if she'd wet the bed - or, rather, Stephanie's face. It was really hot, and Stephanie pulled back, wiped her face with a washcloth, and offered Kelsey the next round of pills. She downed them immediately.

"How many of these are we going to have me- AH!" Kelsey interrupted herself with a scream of pleasure as Stephanie's tongue began to tantalize her clit again. "Fuck fuck fuuuck…"

With that, her body kept on expanding. Her frame softened even further, thickening mostly around her ass and thighs, though a healthy amount went to her breasts, her belly, and her face.

"Wow," Kelsey observed as she looked at herself in the vanity mirror. "I really am fat, now."

"It's just the beginning, sweetheart," Stephanie whispered, and Kelsey took her next set of pills.

"Oh, my god," Kelsey breathed, watching as her stomach bulged in her very hands, filling out into a massive overhanging belly. Her lap was entirely obscured by her stomach at this point, and she looked like a profound little brown-haired Buddha.

"There we go," Stephanie comforted her, "You're finally starting to round out a little."

So saying, Stephanie gave Kelsey her fourth dose, and provided encouragement with her tongue running all around Kelsey's taut navel.

With this additional forty-odd pounds, a fine and sumptuous double-belly formed - she had grown too fat for her small torso to accommodate all of her squishiness in one single belly.

"Damn," Kelsey murmured, looking nearly faint as she saw herself in the mirror, "I can't believe it. I'm really enormous."

"Now just one more, dearie," Stephanie beseeched her, and with a hesitant breath, Kelsey swallowed the remaining pills. And then she surveyed the damage with grim amusement.

In less than an hour, she had ballooned two hundred pounds larger than she walked in the door. Now she wasn't entirely sure if she *could* walk out the door, since her weight gain was so massive she hadn't had time to build up strength in her legs. Her waist's circumference was now approximately more than her height of sixty-six inches. Her belly hung so low, practically to her knees. And her breasts had become enormous, resting weight of around twenty pounds each on their own, judging by their heft.

And despite it all, there was Stephanie, frantically eating her out, desperately sucking her dry like marrow from chicken bones.

"God, you're so fucking hot," Stephanie moaned, and with a sudden burst of inspiration, she noticed there were a few pills left. "Bon voyage," she crowed, and lay back as they did their magic.

Forty pounds on her frame wasn't quite as big a deal as it was on Kelsey, not by a long shot - but her third belly became even more pronounced, and she hiccupped so cutely.

"Okay," Stephanie confirmed, "now I know what *that's* like."

"That was so damn hot," Kelsey breathed, and she pressed a frantic kiss into Stephanie's plump lips. "Look at you. I wonder if you can even fit in your car now."

"Hm," Stephanie moaned, and grinned. "Well, we definitely won't once we've had some dinner."

"Oh, I guess I am starving," Kelsey murmured. And as Stephanie heaved herself out of bed and waddled to the kitchen, Kelsey followed with ambling, unsteady steps, like a newborn fawn learning to walk.

Stephanie began to gather together some tuna salad, watermelon, coleslaw, and marinated mushrooms (a perfectly decadent cold dinner). As she watched Kelsey attempt uselessly to assist her in preparations, she couldn't help but smirk in pride and excitement. Which expression was met with Kelsey's bright-eyed and eager grin.

Oh yes, Stephanie confirmed to herself. This was going to be so much *fucking* fun.

ABOUT THE AUTHOR

Molly Weisser is a BBW in her own right brimming with self-love and positive sexual energy that she seeks to spread throughout the world. Her books have an international following that extends across every major continent. She lives in a major city on the east coast of the United States, and enjoys a kinky, fat-positive, polyamorous lifestyle. She enjoys large people of all genders and sexual predispositions, and especially enjoys cuddles.

She believes in Health at Every Size and tries to straddle the real-life complicated experience of being a hard-wired feedism kinkster while also wanting to be a happy and healthy plus-size person. She enjoys writing fanfiction, watching movies, and spending time with her girlfriend.

You can find out more about her ongoing and upcoming works on her Facebook page: https://www.facebook.com/MollyBBW/

For a list of her other publications available for purchase, please check out her author page on Amazon:
http://www.amazon.com/author/mollyweisser

She also maintains a presence of Patreon:
https://www.patreon.com/mollyweisser/